Ice City

Written by Roderick Hunt

Illustrated by Alex Brychta

OXFORD
UNIVERSITY PRESS

Read these words

puss	ice
dress	prince
glass	palace
geese	nurse

Mum and Dad took the children to
Ice City.

"So this is Ice City," said Biff.
"What a place."

"It's all made of ice," said Chip.
"This is so exciting."

They went to the Ice Palace. It had
scenes from fairy tales. They were
made out of ice.

"I can see Puss in Boots,"
said Kipper.

"And here is Mother Goose," said
Mum. "Look at all the geese."

"Guess who this is," said Biff.
"Look at her dress."

"See. It's Cinderella and the Ugly Sisters," said Biff.

"The sisters were not nice to Cinderella," said Kipper.

They went skating.
Kipper did not like skating.

Oh no! Biff hit Chip in the face.
It was an accident.

A nurse looked at Chip's face.
"It's fine," she said.

"We all need some dinner," said
Dad. "Let's go and eat."

They went to The Ice House.
It was made of ice.

They had a slice of pizza and
some juice.

"Even my glass is made of ice,"
said Kipper.

After dinner, Dad took the
children on the bobsleigh ride.

"The bobsleigh will bump,"
said Dad.

The ride began. "It's like a real bobsleigh," said Kipper.

"It's exciting," called Biff.
"It's like a real race," said Chip.

The sun began to go down. "Look at Ice City in the sunset," said Mum.

"It's all lit up by the sun,"
said Chip.

The moon rose.
Ice City went silver.

"It's all lit up by the moon," said
Biff. "It looks so peaceful."

"Time for bed," said Dad.

"What a super day," said Biff.

Talk about the story

How can you tell the family is on holiday?

Which fairy tale scenes did the children spot?

Why did Biff say sorry to Chip?

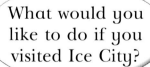

What would you like to do if you visited Ice City?

Missing letters

Find the missing letters by looking back in the story.

Pu__ in boots   Mother Goo__

_inderella   the prin__

Ugly _i_ter